This book belongs to...

For all children with colds, that they may smile even as they sneeze. —C.C.

For my adventurous Mom, with many thanks for an amazing trip to Alaska! —K.B.

Other Dr. Hippo Stories
The Little Elephant with the Big Earache

Peeper Has a Fever

Upcoming books from The Hippocratic Press
Look for Dr. Hippo in upcoming stories: A giraffe with a sore throat
and a moose with loose poops are coming soon!

Ordering information
Order books from your local book retailer, your online book source, or directly from:

The Hippocratic Press

281A Fairhaven Hill Road

Concord, MA 01742

www.hippocraticpress.com

Text and illustrations copyright © The Hippocratic Press, LLC. 2005. All rights reserved.

First American edition 2005 published by The Hippocratic Press.

No part of this book may be reproduced or transmitted in any form or by any means, electronic or mechanical, including photocopying, recording, or by any information storage or retrieval system, without permission in writing from the Publisher. Requests for such permission should be sent to: The Hippocratic Press, 281A Fairhaven Hill Road, Concord, MA 01742.

Charlotte Cowan, M.D. and Katy Bratun assert the right to be identified as the author and the illustrator of this work.

Printed in China.

Library of Congress Control Number: 2005926040

ISBN 0-9753516-3-X

Katie Caught a Cold

by Charlotte Cowan, M.D.   *illustrated by* Katy Bratun

book design by Labor Day Creative

THE HIPPOCRATIC PRESS
CONCORD, MA

"Mom," yelled Katie, "we need to practice some more!"

Her mother smiled.

"Katie, your twirls look great, and the Ice Show's not for five days!"

"I've almost finished your costumes, cubs. You'll be perfect 'Little Teapots!'"

"Achoo," Katie sneezed. "Achoo... ACHOO!!"

"Katie," said her Mom, "sneeze into your sleeve!"

Lara laughed, "Lucky you're not twirling now, Katie: You'd fall for sure!"

"I won't fall," promised Katie. "See you tomorrow!"

"Katie Bear, do you feel all right?" her mother
asked. "You're sniffling and sneezing!"

"I'm okay, Mom. Just cold and shivery from
skating. Come on, Frosty, it's your turn."

After dinner, the cubs had their bedtime
story. "I get to choose tomorrow night,"
said Katie. "Achoo!"

"Here's some water in case you get thirsty, Katie Bear. I hope you feel better in the morning."

"I'll be fine, Mom," said Katie.

Their mother kissed them.

"Good night, little cubs," she whispered.

The next morning, Katie asked, "Mom, are you making apple pie?"

"Can't you smell the cinnamon, Katie? You must be getting stuffed up," said her mother. "Come have breakfast, cutie."

But Katie started to sneeze.
"Ah… Ah… Achoo!"

"Achoo! Achoo!!" She took a breath.

"ACHOO!!"

"Bless you, Katie!" said her Mom. "Now come have breakfast."

Katie answered, "No thanks, I'm not hungry. I'm all stuffy."

She was quiet for a minute. "Hey, Mom, I'm blowing *green* stuff into my tissue."

"That's okay, Katie. Go sit by the fire and I'll get my thermometer."

"Katie Bear, I know you don't like having your temperature taken. But it's helpful to know if you have a fever before I call Dr. Hippo."

"Katie's temperature is normal," said her Mom, "but she's still too sick for school. After breakfast, I'll call Dr. Hippo to see what he thinks about the 'green stuff.'"

"Good idea," said Daddy Bear. "I'll take Frosty to school."

Katie thought, "I want to go, too."

Then she listened to her Mom.

"Dr. Hippo, Katie's sneezing and blowing *yellowish-green mucous.*" She paused. "No, she doesn't have a fever."

Katie imagined Dr. Hippo's office and the things he always said.

❧ "How's the cutest cub in the whole North Pole?"
❧ "Goodness how you've grown, my friend!"
❧ "Keep on twirling, Little Bear!"

She smiled.

"Yes," her mother said, "I understand now: Green mucous is fine and will go away without antibiotics. I never knew it could be part of a *viral* infection. Goodness!"

She paused. "If Katie gets a fever after the first couple of days, *of course* I'll call you back."

She put down her pen. "No medicine for her stuffy nose? That's a surprise! But I can focus on extra liquids and rest. Thank you so much, Dr. Hippo."

"You're very welcome," he said. "Please tell Katie that I hope she feels better soon and I'll look for her at the Show!"

"Here's some juice, cutie," offered her Mom. "Dr. Hippo said you should stop *sneezing like a snowstorm*—or you'll make everyone sick!"

Katie laughed. "But can I be in the Ice Show, Mom?"

"We'll see. He thinks you'll feel better in a couple of days."

"Katie, let's make scarves this morning and then bake cookies after your nap," suggested her mother.

"Achoo," sneezed Katie. "Achoo! Achoo!!" She blew her nose and said, "Let's sew swirls onto the scarves, Mom, like steam."

Katie sneezed for a few days and then, one morning, jumped out of bed. "The Ice Show's *today!*" she exclaimed.

"Eat your breakfast, Katie," urged her Mom. "I made cocoa to keep you warm."

"And I made you a picture for good luck," chimed in Frosty.

Katie smiled. "Thanks, Frost," she said.

"Do you think we have everything?" asked Father Bear.
"Did you pack your skates?"

"Got them, Dad." Katie grinned. "We're ready to go!"

The Show went on and on and then Frosty shouted, "Listen! The song of the 'Little Teapots!' It's Katie's turn!"

"I'm worried about Katie and her new cough," whispered her Mom to Daddy Bear. "But Dr. Hippo told me not to worry unless it lasted longer than two weeks or had a fever with it."

"Let's give it some time," he replied. "Dr. Hippo thought Katie could skate today. Let's watch!"

"Look, Mom," said
Frosty, "Katie's twirling
and she's... okay!"

They stood up and waved
at the cubs. "Hooray for
the 'Little Teapots!'"
they shouted.

The crowd grew quiet as Grandfather Walrus
led the judges onto the ice.

"Cubs, you all deserve *huge* bear hugs for your
wonderful costumes and skating," he said.

"And this year's North Star goes to the 'Little Teapots' for their terrific teamwork!" Grandfather Walrus beamed.

Dr. Hippo added: "I'm so glad to see Katie back to her old self: Instead of sneezes, she's filled with smiles!"

The photographer smiled. "Are you cubs ready for the team picture? Just say '*sneeze*,' please!"